**FRIENDS
OF ACPL**

HOLIDAY COLLECTION

O9-ABI-248

3 1833 05809 8424

11/09

For Patricia, Oréo, and the Pépélia
— J-P. A-V.

To Basile
— O. T.

First published in the United States in 2009 by Chronicle Books LLC.

Text © 2006 by Jean-Philippe Arrou-Vignod.
Illustrations © 2006 by Olivier Tallec.
Translation © 2009 by Chronicle Books LLC.
Originally published in France in 2006 by Gallimard Jeunesse under the title
Le Noël de Rita et Machin.
All rights reserved. No part of this book may be reproduced in any form
without written permission from the publisher.
North American type design by Natalie Davis.
Typeset in The Serif Semi Light.
Manufactured in China.

Library of Congress Cataloging-in-Publication Data
Arrou-Vignod, Jean-Philippe, 1958–
[Noël de Rita et Machin. English]
Rita and Whatsit's Christmas / by Jean-Philippe Arrou-Vignod ; illustrated by
Olivier Tallec.
p. cm.
"Originally published in France in 2006 by Gallimard Jeunesse under the
title *Le Noël de Rita et Machin.*"
Summary: Rita and her sometime talking dog, Whatsit, prepare for the
arrival of Santa Claus on Christmas Eve.
ISBN 978-0-8118-6681-1
[1. Christmas—Fiction. 2. Dogs—Fiction.] I. Tallec, Olivier, ill. II. Title.
PZ7.A74339Ri 2009
[E]—dc22
2008048646

10 9 8 7 6 5 4 3 2 1

Chronicle Books LLC
680 Second Street, San Francisco, California 94107

www.chroniclekids.com

By JEAN-PHILIPPE ARROU-VIGNOD Illustrated by OLIVIER TALLEC

chronicle books · san francisco

Tonight is Christmas Eve.
But there's still so much to do!

Quick! Rita and Whatsit write a letter to Santa.

Whatsit doesn't want much:

a chewy ball,

a police dog uniform,

some dog biscuits,
some cat crackers,
a treadmill,
Professor Poodle's new book
How to Train Your Human in 12 Easy Steps,
. . . and about a hundred other things.

"Whatsit!" says Rita. "That's not how you decorate a Christmas tree! I need ornaments, garlands, and some *help*. Now behave, or else!"

Whatsit has his own little tree. It has a garland
of sausages, slices of salami, and some bologna.
It smells wonderful.

Quick, to the kitchen!
Rita is making her specialty:
no-bake Christmas cake with
cocoa and canned pumpkin.

It looks delicious.
Rita and Whatsit put it outside
as a snack for Santa, with some
carrots for his reindeer.

Then Whatsit howls "Silent Night," and Rita conducts.
It's a special private concert.

But Whatsit prefers rock 'n' roll.
He likes the outfit better.

It's almost bedtime. Rita has a stocking, but she
likes to think big. She puts all her shoes out, too.

Whatsit puts out a slipper he's been chewing.
Most of the flavor is gone.

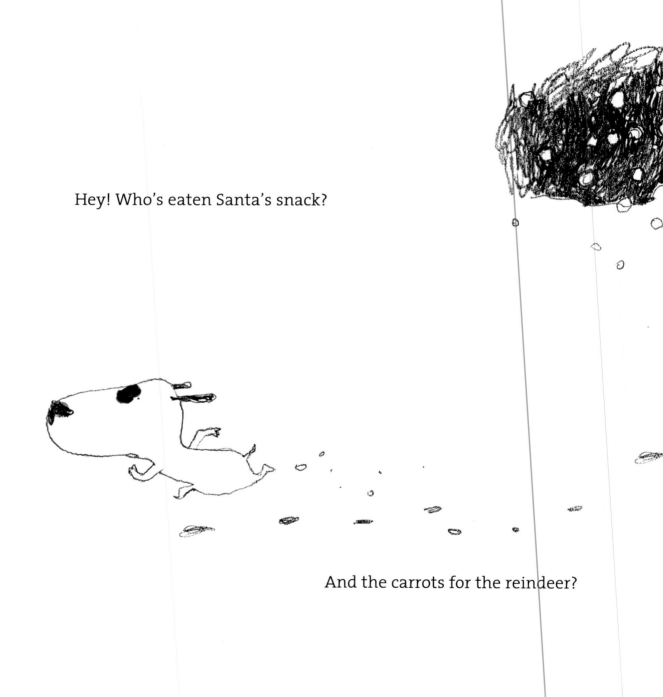

Hey! Who's eaten Santa's snack?

And the carrots for the reindeer?

"Whatsit! You four-legged stomach!
Get back here right now!"

"Time for bed!" say Mom and Dad.
"And no peeking at the tree until
tomorrow morning!"

But it's hard to wait all night
when it's Christmas Eve.

Shh. It's midnight. Everyone but Whatsit is asleep.
Suddenly there's a noise downstairs. And then
another. Someone's in the house!

Whatsit the guard dog will investigate!
Burglars had better watch out for their ankles.

What was that? Whatsit takes a deep breath
and barks his big dog bark.

"Shhhh! Whatsit, what are you barking at?"
Quickly, Rita and Whatsit creep downstairs
in the dark.

But downstairs, everything is quiet.
The visitor has disappeared.
"Oh no! We scared away *Santa Claus*!"

But when they open the living room door, what do they find? Under the twinkling Christmas tree, Santa has left all the presents they could ask for.

All? Well, no. There's just *one* missing (that can't
be wrapped)—a big hug from your best friend.

Merry Christmas, Rita! Merry Christmas, Whatsit!